Sid and the
Cwmhendy
Dog Show

Sid and the Cwmhendy Dog Show

Tanya L. James

Illustrated by
Petra Brown

Pont

To Richard who was always there to listen

To Nic, Simon, Dan and Mum who encouraged
me all the way through

To Sophie, Sid and Nancy – without their doggy
capers there would be no tales to tell!

'Children are made readers on the laps
of their parents.' Emilie Buchwald

First published in 2013 by Pont Books, an imprint of
Gomer Press, Llandysul, Ceredigion, SA44 4JL
www.gomer.co.uk

ISBN 978 1 84851 650 2

A CIP record for this title is available from the British Library.

This book is published with the financial support of the Welsh Books Council.

Printed and bound in Wales at Gomer Press, Llandysul, Ceredigion

Contents

Chapter One

It was a lovely sunny Saturday in the village of Cwmhendy and Sid was having fun in his back garden.

Sid was a very special little dog with short little legs and a curly pig's tail. His tail wagged excitedly as he chased his bright shiny red ball all around the flowerbeds. Oh, how he loved that ball!

He liked to chase it across the lawn, toss it into the air and let it roll to a hidden place. Then he'd put his head to the ground and sniff and sniff with his little black shiny nose until it led him to wherever his ball lay. Then off he'd scamper to play the game again!

Sometimes he'd find his ball under the wheelbarrow or behind the shed, but quite often it would be in the middle of Mum's flowers or Dad's vegetable patch. Then Sid would run – at top speed – through the flowers and vegetables, flattening everything in his path.

Today his ball was lying in the middle of the snapped daffodils and the broken leeks. He tiptoed over the crunchy stalks and picked the ball up gently in his mouth.

Oh, how happy he was to get it back!

Then suddenly Sid paused. He could hear something. He lifted his little ear. The sound was getting closer. He knew those voices. It was Mum. And Dad. They were shouting something. He didn't like those angry voices, so he hid. Sometimes he'd hide under the wheelbarrow but today he hid behind the shed.

'Sid, where are you? Look what you've done to my flowers. All my daffodils are broken,' Mum moaned.

'Oh, Sid, Sid,' Dad shouted. 'Why did you dig up my leeks? They're ruined.'

Sid groaned quietly and then crept gloomily up to Mum and Dad. He sat in front of them, looking up with his big sad eyes.

He hadn't meant to be naughty and spoil the garden. But his shiny red ball was lost and he just had to find it. Oh, Sid was feeling very sorry now.

Chapter Two

Sid walked slowly up towards the house, and crept into the kitchen. He dropped his ball on the floor and hopped into his bed. He sighed heavily as he rested his chin on the side of the basket.

Then he heard a cheery little tune above his head. Someone was humming. It made Sid feel happy. He looked up and saw his most favourite person in the whole world. It was Geraint! Geraint wouldn't be cross.

'Hello, Sid. Come here, boy!' said Geraint.

Sid sprang out of his basket.

Geraint knelt down and hugged and patted the little dog with the short legs and the curly pig's tail. Sid wriggled with excitement. His tail wagged and he barked happily. Oh, he felt so much better. He knew that Geraint would be pleased to see him.

'Calm down, boy. Sit quietly. Now, I want to tell you something. Today is a big day. Shall I tell you why?'

Sid looked up at Geraint and listened carefully.

'Today, Sid, is the day of the Cwmhendy Dog Show. And guess what, boy: I'm going to enter you, because I think that you're in with a big chance of winning.'

'Wow,' thought Sid, Geraint was taking him to a dog show. That sounded like fun.

'Now then, Sid,' said Geraint. 'The first job is to give you a good bath. I'm going to make you look really smart.'

Sid stared in alarm. Had he heard right? Did Geraint just say that he was going to give him a BATH? Oh no, not a bath! He hated having a bath.

Sid's ears dropped and his tail flopped but he followed Geraint into the bathroom.

'I'll put some bubbles in for a treat,' said Geraint. He sang as he filled the bath with bubbly water.

At that moment Sid noticed that Geraint hadn't closed the door. He decided to make his escape. He'd walk slowly, very slowly, towards the door . . . and then run into the garden and hide.

He took his first step . . . then another . . . then whoosh! What was happening? He was swept up into the air by Geraint's strong arms and then gently plopped into the bathwater before he had a chance to escape.

'This is nice, isn't it, Sid?' said Geraint. 'I bet you're enjoying this.'

Sid sat sadly in the water. His fur was wet and he didn't like it at all. He hated having a bath. He absolutely hated it.

The bubbles tickled his nose and made him sneeze and he whined when the water splashed in his eyes. He had to get out of that bath. He had to. But just as he was about to jump up out of the water, quick as a flash, Geraint threw a giant fluffy towel around him.

'Good boy, Sid,' he said. 'Nearly finished. I'm going to rub you dry now.'

'Rub me dry?' thought Sid. 'I don't need to be rubbed dry with a towel. I can shake myself dry, thank you very much.'

Before Geraint had a chance to take cover, Sid began to shake his soaking wet coat. He shook it so hard that poor Geraint was left dripping wet in the middle of the bathroom.

As Geraint brushed the wet hair out of his eyes he noticed Sid sneaking towards the door. 'Hold on a minute, boy,' he said. 'I haven't brushed you yet.'

BRUSH? BRUSH? Oh not the brush! Geraint hadn't said anything about a brush.

Enough was enough. There was no way that Sid was staying in that bathroom a minute longer. He was off. Right now.

And Sid scampered out of the house as fast as his little legs would carry him.

Chapter Three

Sid reached the lawn in record time and quickly rolled onto his back, rubbing his wet fur dry on the muddy grass.

Oh, that felt better! But then he heard a voice calling him.

'Sid? Sid? Where are you, boy?'

Before Sid had a chance to think about where to hide, Geraint was standing there in front of him.

'Oh, Sid!' Geraint couldn't believe the sight that met his eyes. His little white dog with black spots was now a little brown dog with white patches! Geraint shook his head:

'Oh, Sid. What have you done?

Wait, wait! Don't you run!'

'You can't take him to the dog show looking like that, Geraint,' said Dad, coming around the corner of the greenhouse. 'Everyone will laugh.'

'I know, Dad. I'm going to have to give him another bath.'

'I'll come and help you. What time does the show start?'

'Three o'clock,' said Geraint.

'Three o'clock! That doesn't give us much time,' said Dad. 'It's one o'clock now. We'd better get our skates on.'

A very quiet Sid was lifted into the bath for the second time that day. He didn't make a sound when Geraint quickly brushed the mud from his coat but he couldn't wait for the washing to stop. He'd had quite enough of all this bathing. Two baths in one day was just too much.

Geraint scooped him up in a towel and rubbed him dry. Again. Dad stood guard at the door in case Sid tried to escape.

At last he was ready.

Geraint and Dad stood back to admire him. Sid's white fur was now fluffy and clean again and even his black spots shone.

'Fair play, Sid *bach*, *chwarae teg* – you're looking very smart. Very smart indeed,' said Dad. 'Now come on, Geraint. We'd better hurry up. We don't want to be late for the show.'

Geraint put Sid in the back of Dad's car and off they drove to the Cwmhendy show.

Chapter Four

Sid sat up straight as the car pulled out of the drive. He was very proud. He'd never felt so smart.

Then he snuggled down onto the back seat and smiled at his perfect fur. Oh, it smelt so good and felt so clean. Sid thought he looked smart enough to be on TV or even to meet the Queen.

But slowly he began to think that something was missing. Now what could it be?

It was something special. Something that Sid liked a lot.

Then he remembered. He remembered that he'd left his bright shiny red ball back at the house. Oh no. What was he going to play with now?

He looked on the seat for something to chew. Anything would do. But he definitely needed something to chew.

He sniffed and sniffed and looked and looked but the seat was bare.

There was nothing there at all. 'I know,' Sid thought, 'I'll tell Geraint that I've forgotten my ball. He's sure to help me. Yes, Geraint will help me.'

Sid stood on the seat and barked and barked at Geraint to tell him that he'd forgotten to bring his ball.

'What's the matter, boy? Why are you barking? Don't you like it back there?' asked Geraint.

Sid gave him a look. What a daft question! Geraint was so silly sometimes.

Of course he liked the seat. That wasn't the problem. The problem was he'd forgotten his ball. His bright shiny red ball.

'Well, Sid,' said Geraint. 'If you don't like it on the seat, get down onto the floor. It's cooler down there. Go on, boy.'

Sid thought he'd better do as Geraint said. He slid down onto the floor behind the front seat. He lay down, stretched his paws out and laid his head on top of them. He sighed heavily and wondered what to do.

Then, suddenly, he saw something shining under the seat. Mmm, what could it be?

He moved his nose closer, and sniffed and sniffed. It smelt nice.

He dragged it closer with his paw. He wondered what it was. It looked nice too.

He licked it.

Oh, oh, it tasted really nice. Really very nice indeed.

He chewed and chewed it. It was yummy.

Dad looked in the rear view mirror and then across at Geraint. 'Sid's quiet back there, isn't he?'

'I expect he's gone to sleep,' said Geraint.

'You're probably right,' replied Dad.

Sid went on munching and crunching his new toy.

Suddenly the car came to a halt.

'Oh dear,' said Dad. 'Geraint, look. We'll have to wait. Gwyn is moving his cows. They're all over the road.'

'Oh no!' said Geraint. 'We'll be late for the show.'

'No, we've still got ten minutes. We'll get there in time. Don't worry,' said Dad.

Gwyn waved his hand cheerily at Dad and Geraint as he led his cows into the field.

Before long, the road was clear again and off they drove.

In the back of the car, Sid chewed and chewed and chewed.

Suddenly the car was slowing down again. 'I don't believe this!' said Dad.

'What now?' asked Geraint.

'The lights are flashing. The Cwmhendy station gates are closing. We'll have to wait for the train to pass by.'

'We'll be late for the show,' Geraint said unhappily.

'No, don't give up,' said Dad. 'We've still got five minutes.'

Chapter Five

WELCOME TO THE CWMHENDY DOG SHOW!

'Hurrah,' said Dad. 'We've made it.'

It was exactly three o'clock and they'd arrived just in time for the most important dog show in the whole of Wales. The Cwmhendy Dog Show.

Dad quickly parked the car and Geraint jumped out. He couldn't wait to see his fluffy white little dog with the short legs and the curly pig's tail. He opened the door for Sid to jump out. But he was in for a surprise.

When Geraint saw Sid he couldn't believe his eyes.

'Oh, Sid, what have you done? You're all BLUE!'

And he was. Sid was completely BLUE from head to tail. The brightest blue you've ever seen in the whole of your life.

A chewed-up blue pen dropped from Sid's mouth.

He glanced down at his fur. How had it turned this wonderful colour? He quite liked it. He looked different to any other dog he'd ever seen. He was unique.

People would say, 'Look at that incredible blue dog!' Sid looked up happily at Geraint.

But Geraint wasn't happy at all.

He looked very sad.

Very sad indeed.

'Oh, Sid!'

'What's the matter?' asked Dad.

'Come and see,' said Geraint.

Dad walked round to Geraint's side of the car. When he saw Sid, he stopped in his tracks and stood with his mouth wide open. He didn't say a word. It was as though his mouth didn't work any more.

Sid could see tears in Geraint's eyes. He looked so sad. Poor Geraint. What was wrong? Didn't they like his new blue look?

Dad picked up the chewed blue pen. He looked down at Sid and said, 'What are we going to do now? We can't enter a blue dog in the show, can we, Sid?'

'Oh, Dad, can't we clean him up with something?' pleaded Geraint.

'Well, let's have a look in the car. There might be an old blanket or something to rub him with,' said Dad.

Time was running out. Dad and Geraint searched the car quickly but found nothing they could use to rub Sid clean. They looked at each other sadly and shrugged their shoulders.

'Come on, Geraint,' said Dad. 'Let's go home. We'll enter him into next year's show instead.'

Then Geraint spotted something white and woolly in the back of the car. 'Hey, look what I found!' he said. 'It's an old blanket.' Then he rubbed and rubbed the little dog with the soft warm wool, but Sid was still quite blue.

'Oh dear,' said Geraint. 'Look at the blanket. It's turned blue.'

Dad held it up and shook his head angrily. 'Oh, Geraint! That wasn't a blanket. It was my best Aran sweater. Gran knitted it specially for me. It's . . . it's ruined.'

'Oh, Dad. I'm really, really sorry,' said Geraint. 'Perhaps Mum will be able to wash it.'

'Come on, we're going home,' growled Dad crossly. 'Hop in the car, Sid!'

Chapter Six

But, but, Sid so wanted to go to the show. He had been getting ready for this all day. He'd had two baths, yes, two horrid baths, and now Dad had decided – just because he was blue – that he wasn't allowed to go to the show. It wasn't fair. It wasn't fair at all.

There was nothing wrong with looking different to all the other dogs. He thought he looked amazing, unique and very special. Very special indeed. He felt like a winner.

Sid decided there and then that he was going to enter the show. He'd make Dad and Geraint see that he really was a winner. It didn't matter that he was a different colour. He was still a very special little dog.

Sid ran like he'd never run before. He dodged people's legs and skirted around corners, until finally he screeched to a halt at the end of a line of dogs. They were standing very quietly by the show ring.

Over the loudspeaker a voice announced that the Cwmhendy Dog Show was about to begin.

'Phew!' Sid sighed happily. He'd arrived in the nick of time. What a relief! He'd made it.

Just wait until Mrs Rhiannon Rhys, the lady judge, met him. Was she in for a treat! She was about to meet a true original, one of its kind, the one and only blue Jack Russell dog in Wales. He grinned as he thought this must be her luckiest day.

Geraint and Dad rushed to the ringside, their eyes searching frantically for Sid. Where was he? Then Geraint pointed at the line of dogs and shouted, 'Look, Dad. There's Sid! He's over there, next to that little black poodle. Sid! Sid!'

Everybody turned to look at Geraint.

'Shh, Geraint,' said Dad. 'Everybody's staring. Yes, I can see him.'

'Shall I go and get him, Dad?'

'Well the show has already started. We'd better just stay here and watch!'

'OK,' said Geraint. He looked at the other dogs. They were quite an impressive lot. They were all very smart. Their coats had been brushed until they shone. Geraint could hardly look at Sid. His coat looked even bluer than it had before. He sighed. What was he going to do?

He watched as his little dog stood proudly with his head held high. Sid didn't seem to mind being blue at all. In fact he seemed to rather like it. Oh, he was a funny little dog.

At that moment, Mrs Rhiannon Rhys began inspecting each dog in the row . . .

Noodle the Poodle, who had a terrific curly coat,

Doug the Pug, whose nose wrinkled to perfection

and Dafydd the Dachshund with long silky ears that shone as they flapped in the breeze.

Mrs Rhiannon Rhys bent down to inspect each and every dog, and looked closely at their coats through her enormous black spectacles.

And then she arrived in front of Sid. She stopped and looked and stared. She removed her spectacles and rubbed them clean.

She replaced them on her nose and stooped a little closer and then moved closer still.

The crowd fell silent as Mrs Rhiannon Rhys got ready to make an announcement. Suddenly her voice boomed out: 'BUT HE'S BLUE. HE'S COMPLETELY BLUE FROM HEAD TO TAIL. HE'S BLUE ALL OVER.'

Chapter Seven

Mrs Rhiannon Rhys, who'd judged more dog shows than anybody else in Wales, stumbled to a chair. She looked confused.

'Well I never. In all my days I've never seen a blue dog before. I'm so glad I came today.'

The crowd began to clap and laugh. They too were amazed to see their first blue dog, and in Cwmhendy of all places. What a treat!

Sid was pleased too. The crowd cheered and called his name. He felt very important. Very important indeed. He stood a bit straighter and held his head a little higher. He was so very proud of himself.

The crowd suddenly went quiet. What was happening now?

Sid watched as the owners paraded their dogs in front of Mrs Rhiannon Rhys.

She sighed loudly as Noodle the Poodle pulled on his lead.

She edged away from Doug the Pug as he growled at her. Growling indeed! At Mrs Rhiannon Rhys, the champion Welsh judge.

Well, well!

She shook her head at Dafydd the Dachshund when he refused to budge.

Mrs Rhiannon Rhys leaned back in her chair as Sid, the little dog with the short legs and the curly pig's tail, walked up very smartly on his own. He stood in front of the lady judge who also happened to have terrific BLUE hair. Just like his.

Sid felt very smart. Very smart indeed.

He sat and gave a surprised Mrs Rhys his paw.

Mrs Rhiannon Rhys smiled warmly at the little dog.

And then she said, 'The winner of the best-behaved dog category is . . .

the little blue dog

with the short legs

and the curly pig's tail.

He's such a super incredible dog, I'm sure his name must be S.I.D., or perhaps even S.B.I.D. – the SUPER BLUE INCREDIBLE DOG. I just love that shade of blue, my dear. It's just like mine! Well done, Sid.'

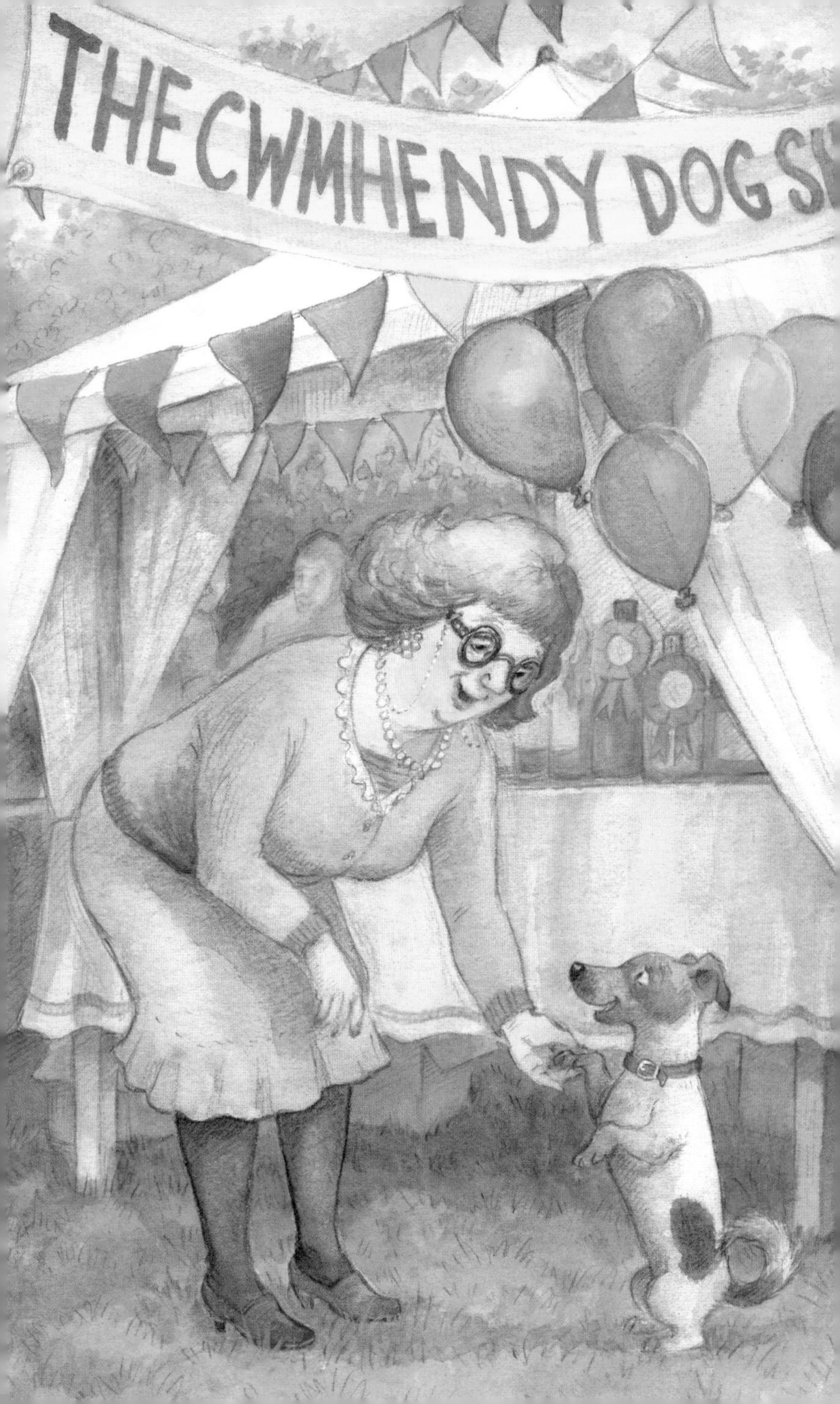
THE CWMHENDY DOG S

Yes, Sid was the winner.

He won £25. Yes, £25.

Geraint was so proud of him.

He spent Sid's winnings on a new Aran jumper for Dad . . . and . . .

the biggest bottle of doggy shampoo you've ever seen.

From the Author

My first job as a waitress, when I was seventeen years old, was sadly cut short when I served a full trout dinner onto the lap of the Chair of the local golf club.

After this first venture into the adult world of work I qualified as a nursery nurse and have worked in education as a teaching assistant for most of my career.

I live in west Wales with my husband Richard, three sons, three dogs (including Sid, of course), and a pair of cheeky gerbils.

My love of children's literature, coupled with a deep sense of commitment to bring the world of reading to young people of all abilities, has been the inspiration to write my first children's book.

My ambition is to create stories that children want to read.

Best wishes

All About Sid

Little did Tanya know on the day she collected Sid from a small farm near the Preseli Mountains how much he would change her life!

Sid's a lovable little dog with a huge character.

His hobbies are playing with his ball, going on long muddy walks and curling up in front of a roaring log fire with his doggy friends Sophie and Nancy.

His many antics and adventures have inspired Tanya to write this story. Sid hopes that you have enjoyed reading the book as much as Tanya enjoyed writing it.